Islands of the Pacific

Cameron Macintosh

Contents

Islands of the Pacific

The Pacific Ocean

The Pacific Ocean is the world's largest ocean. Asia and Australia are located to the west of the Pacific Ocean, and North and South America are on its east. The Pacific Ocean is so large, it is bigger than all of Earth's islands and continents put together, and it is about twice as big as Earth's other great ocean, the Atlantic Ocean.

The Pacific Ocean also includes a number of seas, or bodies of water that are fully or partially surrounded by land, such as the Coral Sea and the Sulu Sea.

The Pacific Ocean

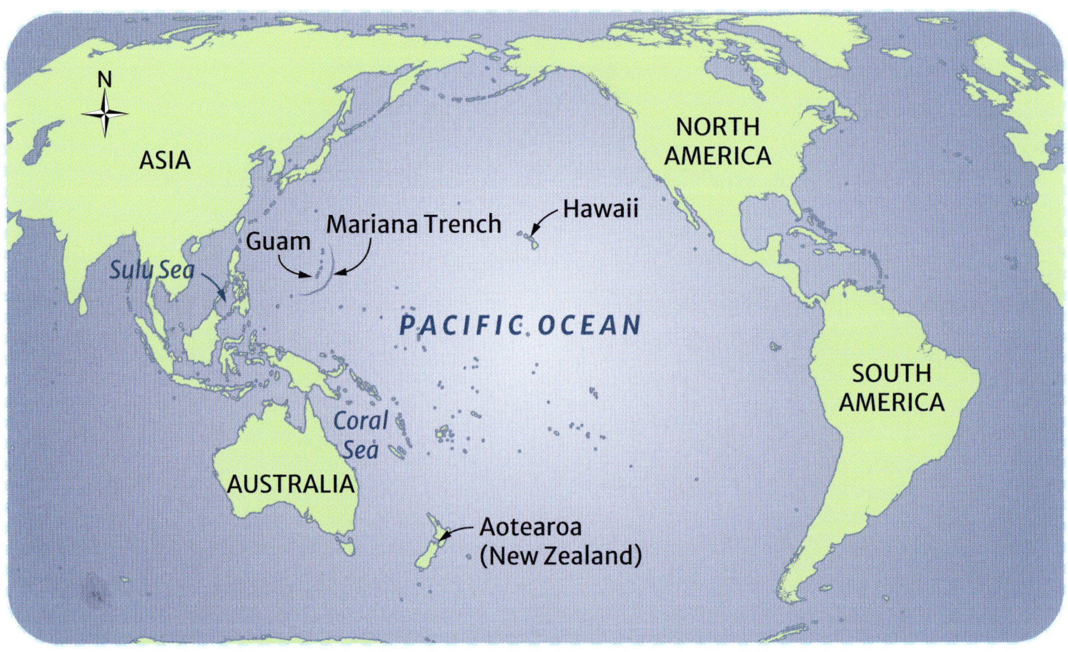

Palau, a country in the Pacific, has hundreds of islands that were pushed up out of the ocean.

As well as being the world's biggest ocean, the Pacific Ocean is also the deepest. The deepest known point is the Mariana Trench, which has a depth of just over 11 kilometres.

There are between 20 000 and 30 000 islands in the Pacific Ocean. Some of these islands were formed by eruptions from volcanoes. Others were formed by movements in Earth's **crust**, which pushed areas of the crust upwards.

Although there are thousands of islands in the Pacific Ocean, most of them are too small to be **inhabited**. Most of the inhabited islands are found in three regions: Polynesia, Micronesia and Melanesia. These regions are grouped by geography and by the cultural similarities of the people who live in them.

The Regions of Polynesia, Micronesia and Melanesia

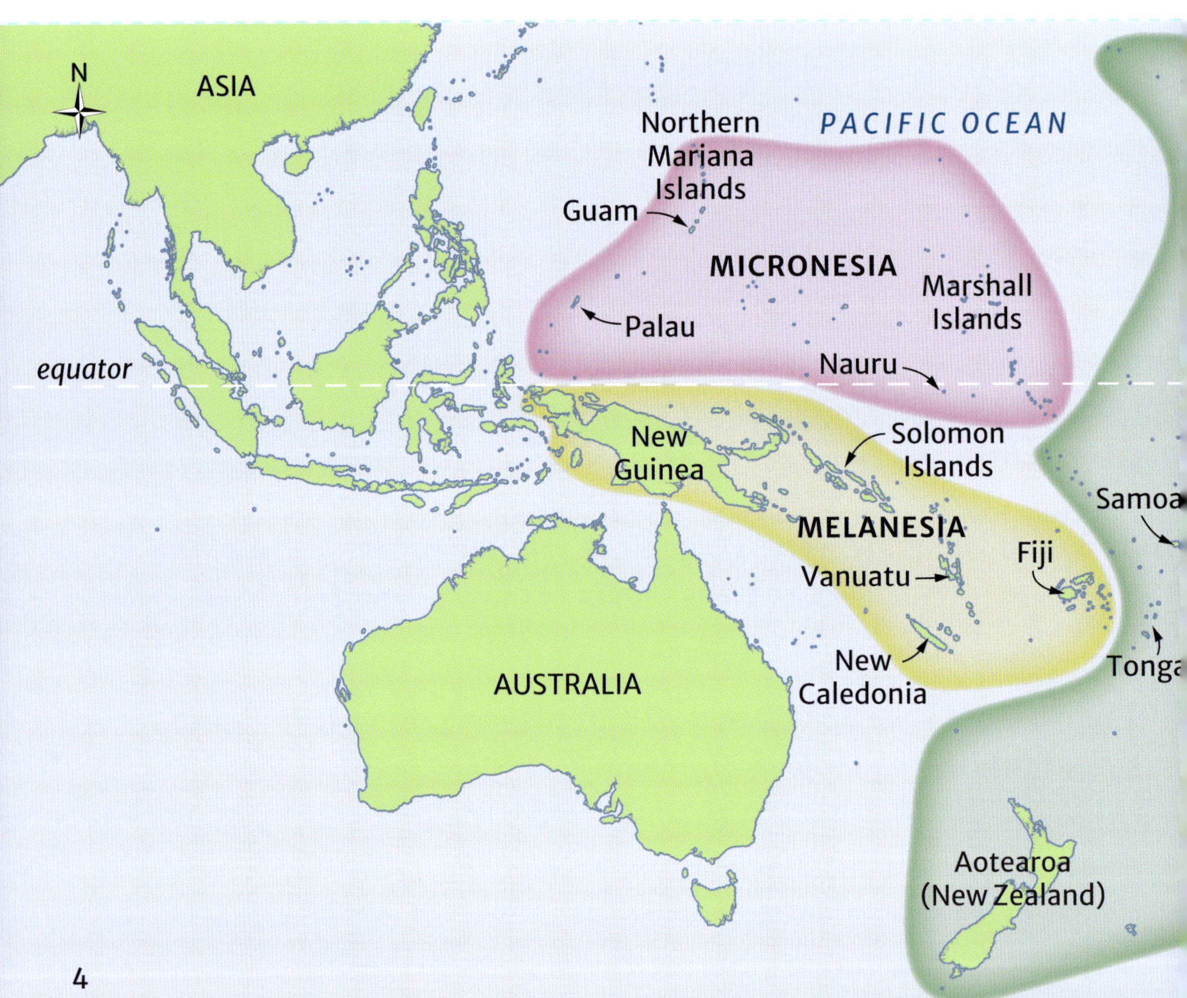

Melanesia is located north of Australia and includes a large area from New Guinea to Fiji. Micronesia is located north of Melanesia. Most of its islands are smaller than Melanesia's, but it covers an area of similar size. Polynesia is located to the east of Melanesia and Micronesia, and is by far the largest of the three regions.

Many of these islands are grouped near the equator, which means they tend to have warm, humid weather most of the year.

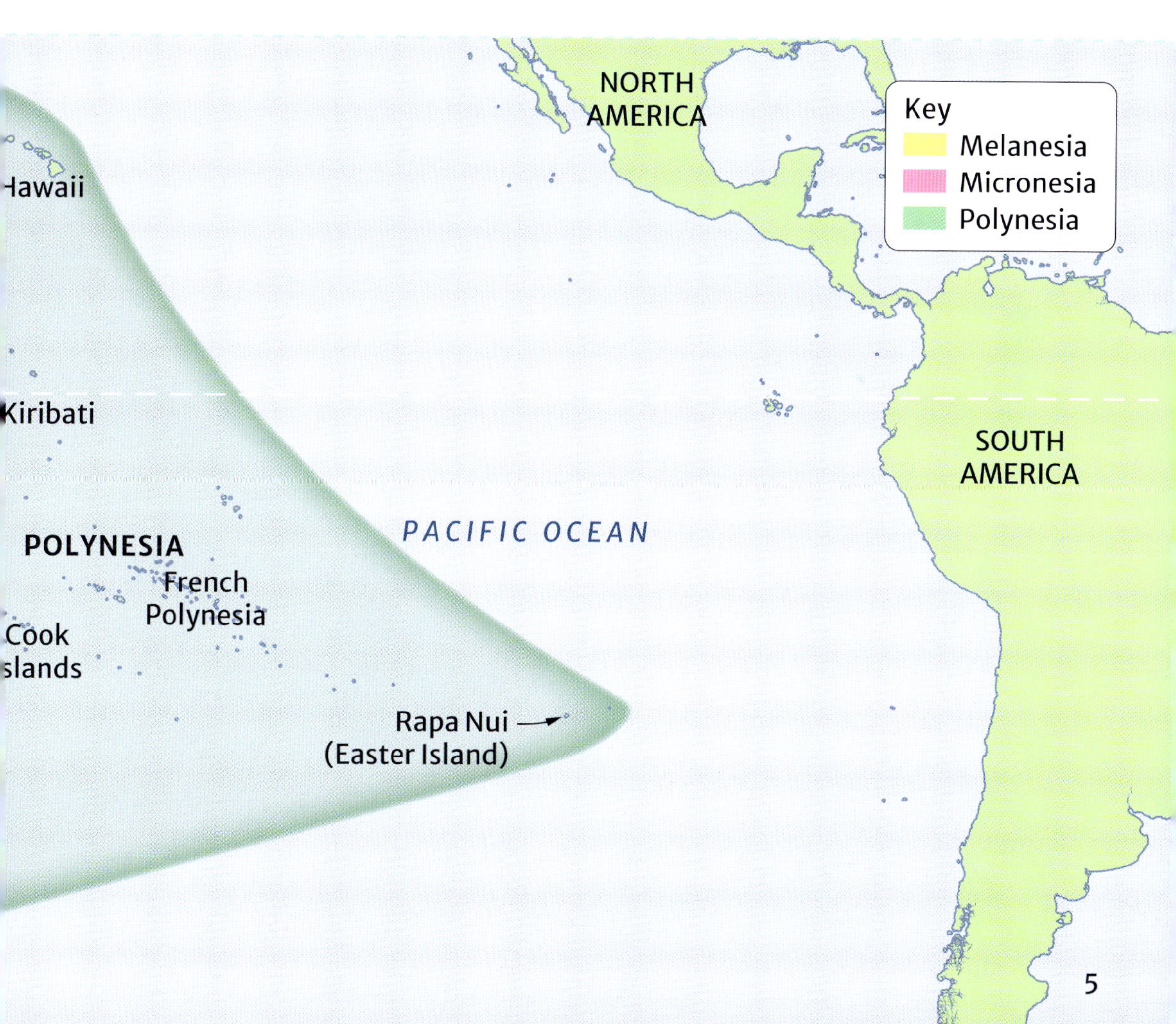

The people of Polynesia, Micronesia and Melanesia share a wide range of cultures and languages. Approximately 1500 different languages are spoken throughout these regions. Many of these languages have similarities as a result of people migrating from island to island over the centuries.

a craftsperson creating a wood carving in French Polynesia

a man playing a bamboo instrument on New Guinea, in Melanesia

a traditional dance in Tahiti, in Polynesia

These island regions have been deeply affected in recent centuries by the arrival of European **colonisers**. French colonisers in particular took control of many Pacific islands in the 1800s. When French colonisers noticed the similarities and differences between the cultures and languages of the islands' inhabitants, they gave the regions the names we use for them today.

In addition to France, countries such as Great Britain, the USA, the Netherlands, Japan and Germany also attempted to take control of much of the area in the late 1800s and early 1900s. Some Pacific islands are still under the control of these colonising powers. For example, Hawaii in Polynesia is now a state of the USA. Another example is French Polynesia, which has been a territory of France since 1842, though it now manages most of its own affairs.

This illustration shows some local Polynesian people in the Marquesas Islands confronting French sailors as they land in 1890.

Polynesia

The largest region in the Pacific Ocean, Polynesia, is often referred to as the Polynesian Triangle due to its shape. Aotearoa (pronounced *ah-oh-teh-ah-roh-ah*), also known as New Zealand, is located in the south-western corner, Hawaii in the northern corner and Rapa Nui (pronounced *rah-puh noo-ee*), also known as Easter Island, in the eastern corner.

Map of Polynesia

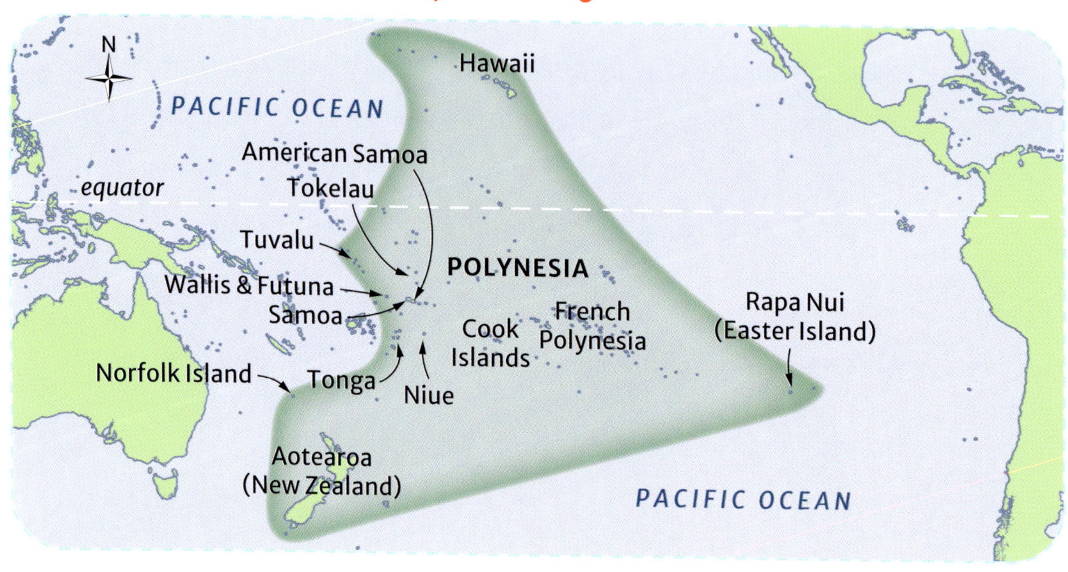

The name "Polynesia" comes from Greek words meaning "many islands". Polynesia contains more than 1000 islands, including volcanic islands and atolls, which are ring-shaped reefs or islands that usually have a lagoon inside. There are huge distances between many of Polynesia's islands.

There are four **independent** countries in Polynesia: Aotearoa, Tonga, Tuvalu and Samoa. Aotearoa is by far the largest country in Polynesia, and it has the largest population – just over five million people. Polynesia also includes many islands that are **administered** by foreign countries. For example, the USA administers American Samoa, Chile administers Rapa Nui and France administers French Polynesia, as well as the islands of Wallis and Futuna. Another example is Norfolk Island, which is a territory of Australia. Other islands such as Tokelau (pronounced *toe-kuh-lau*), Niue (pronounced *nee-oo-ay*) and the Cook Islands govern themselves, but their people are **citizens** of Aotearoa.

Aotearoa is the largest independent country in Polynesia.

The People of Polynesia

Historians believe that the islands of Polynesia were discovered by people from islands near Papua New Guinea who ventured onto the ocean in canoes. These canoes, known as "outrigger" canoes, were able to travel long distances because they had two **hulls**, which made them more stable in rough seas. The islands of Aotearoa (New Zealand) were the last Polynesian islands to be discovered by humans, around 800 years ago.

This painting shows islanders in large and small outrigger canoes meeting Dutch explorers

Today, a **diverse** range of people live on the islands of Polynesia, with a total population of around seven million. The largest Polynesian group is the Māori, who were the first inhabitants of Aotearoa. About 30 different languages are spoken throughout Polynesia, with many similarities between them.

Polynesian culture has been influenced by the close relationship between its people and the sea. Polynesians have always been highly skilled sailors, which allowed them to cross vast areas of the ocean to discover and settle new islands in the region.

A group of students from Aotearoa perform a traditional dance.

A popular game throughout Polynesia is kilikiti (pronounced *ke-le-kitty*), which was invented in Samoa. Kilikiti is similar to cricket but uses a special ball made of rubber from a tree. The bat is shaped like a Samoan club, with a triangle shape on the bottom.

Main Industries

The biggest industries in Polynesia are tourism, fishing and farming, particularly the farming of coconuts for coconut oil. Pearl farming is another important industry, as is the sale of traditional handicrafts such as baskets and necklaces. Many parts of Polynesia are also supported by foreign aid, which is the supply of money, goods or services from one country to another.

shell necklaces made in French Polynesia

One of Polynesia's unique attractions is found on Rapa Nui. Hundreds of stone statues with large faces, called moai (pronounced *mo-eye*), are found across the island. For many years, their creation was a mystery. Archaeologists now believe the Rapa Nui sculptors carved the statues in a **quarry** on the island, then moved them into position on stone platforms.

Environmental Concerns

Polynesia is facing many environmental problems, particularly as a result of climate change. In Tuvalu, for example, rising ocean levels are swamping small islands and causing coastal **erosion**. Smaller islands are in danger of being completely submerged within a few decades. Sea creatures are also under threat because climate change is causing **coral bleaching**. This reduces their available food supply, as coral is eaten by some creatures and provides a habitat for prey. In some places, overfishing by people from other countries threatens many fish species and causes food supply problems for the local people.

Waves threaten to flood an island in Tuvalu as a result of climate change.

Micronesia

Micronesia is a group of about 2000 small islands to the north of Melanesia. Most of Micronesia's islands are in the Northern **Hemisphere**, which means they lie north of the equator. Most of the islands in Micronesia are made up of the remains of coral reefs, while some were formed by volcanic eruptions.

Map of Micronesia

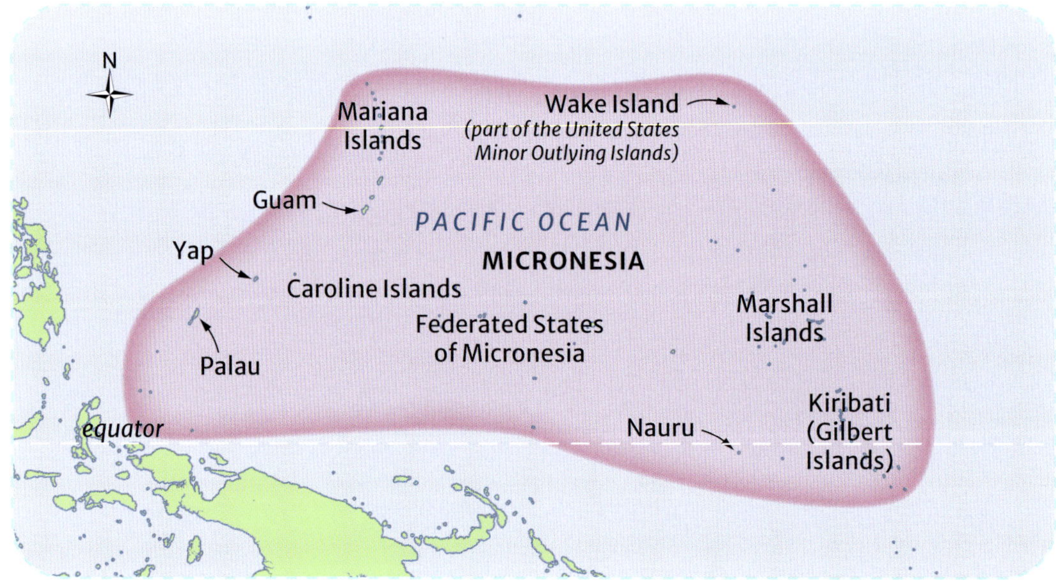

The name "Micronesia" comes from Greek words meaning "small islands". Most of Micronesia is made up of four main archipelagos, which are groups or chains of islands. These four archipelagos are called the Mariana, Caroline, Marshall and Gilbert Islands. There are many other small islands in the region that are not part of these archipelagos.

Micronesia includes Guam, part of Kiribati (the Gilbert Islands), the Marshall Islands, the Federated States of Micronesia, Nauru, the Northern Mariana Islands, Palau and the United States Minor Outlying Islands. Some of these places, such as Nauru, Palau and the Federated States of Micronesia, are independent nations. This means that they have their own government and are not ruled by other countries. Other islands in the region are territories of other nations. For example, the Northern Mariana Islands are partially governed by the USA.

The largest island in Micronesia is Guam. Guam was formed by a volcano and is surrounded by coral reefs. Guam is a US territory, which means that it is largely governed by the USA, although it does have its own governor and **legislature**. It is home to an important military base for the USA.

the city of Dededo in Guam, the largest island in Micronesia

The People of Micronesia

In total, about 500 000 people live in Micronesia, which makes it the least populated Pacific region.

The people of Micronesia are generally divided into two main cultural groups: the low-islanders and the high-islanders. The low-islanders, from coral islands such as Kiribati and the Marshall Islands, usually live on atolls. They have developed excellent seafaring skills over the centuries, particularly fishing techniques, which helped them find food long ago. These skills are still used by many Micronesian people today. The high-islanders, from islands formed by volcanoes, had more food resources at hand, so they generally did not need to travel far from their islands.

The people living on the island of Yap in Micronesia have a very unique form of **currency** – large round stones, often as tall as a fully grown adult. These stones have been used as money for hundreds of years. Although the island's main currency today is the US dollar, these stones are still used in all sorts of important trades, such as the sale of land.

Manra Island in Kiribati is an atoll with a lagoon in the middle.

Guam was formed by a volcano, and it has high mountains in the south.

Main Industries

The people of Micronesia make a living from farming crops such as tomatoes, melons and coconuts. Many people also make a living from fishing. Tourism is important to the economies of the region, too. Palau in particular offers visitors great opportunities for snorkelling and scuba diving.

The mining of phosphate, a type of salt, has long been an important industry, particularly in Nauru. Like other Pacific regions, foreign aid also contributes to the economies of many parts of Micronesia.

Locals catch fish in the Caroline Islands.

A popular tourist attraction in Micronesia is Jellyfish Lake in Palau. This inland lake, full of spectacular golden jellyfish and moon jellyfish, is a popular location for snorkelling. The jellyfish do not sting, so it is safe to swim among them.

Environmental Concerns

The people of Micronesia are also facing environmental challenges as a result of climate change. As in other parts of the Pacific, rising ocean levels threaten to swamp low-lying areas. This also increases the risk of damage from tsunamis, erosion and **salinisation**. As well as being harmful to the people of Micronesia, these problems also threaten many fish and animal species, including the region's coral reefs.

Dead coral can be found on the coast of Guam as a result of climate change.

Melanesia

Melanesia is a region in the southern Pacific Ocean, to the south of Micronesia. It includes the islands of Vanuatu, Fiji, New Caledonia, the Solomon Islands and Papua New Guinea. These are all independent nations, except for New Caledonia, which is governed by France.

Map of Melanesia

an island in Kimbe Bay, Papua New Guinea

a coral reef in New Caledonia

Most of the islands in Melanesia are small coral islands or atolls. Melanesia also contains many coral reefs. The region also includes some large islands, the biggest of which is New Guinea, made up of the nation of Papua New Guinea and West Papua, which is part of Indonesia.

The People of Melanesia

Today, about 11 million people live in Melanesia, with the majority of the population living in Papua New Guinea. Most of the people in Melanesia are thought to be descended from the ancestors of present-day people of New Guinea.

The Melanesian peoples are very diverse, with a wide range of languages spoken across the region's islands. For example, more than 800 different languages are spoken on the island of New Guinea alone. Many of these languages are now in danger of being permanently lost, because many New Guineans now speak English or Tok Pisin, which is a combination of local and European languages.

Before colonisation, Melanesian cultures did not have written forms of their languages. It was extremely important that the people shared their region's history and stories by word of mouth to ensure that they would not be forgotten.

A child and their grandfather sit together during a community gathering in Papua New Guinea.

Masks are an important feature of cultural life in many parts of Melanesia. Elaborately decorated masks are used in ceremonies and festivals in places such as Papua New Guinea, Vanuatu and New Caledonia.

a colourful mask from Vanuatu

Children from Papua New Guinea take an outrigger canoe out from their tropical island.

Wind farms in New Caledonia contribute to the island's renewable energy.

In recent decades, ecotourism has become an important industry in Melanesia. Local people have developed tours, walking trails and special expeditions to show tourists the natural beauty of their islands in ways that do minimal harm to the environment. Tourists are then given the opportunity to support local conservation projects.

Main Industries

The people of Melanesia make a living from tourism, farming, fishing and mining. In Papua New Guinea, the mining of metals such as gold, nickel, silver and copper employs many people. Foreign aid is also important to many parts of Melanesia. In recent years, some countries, such as Vanuatu and New Caledonia, have worked hard to develop large-scale renewable energy industries, including solar and wind farms, as well as producing fuel from coconut oil.

Environmental Concerns

Similar to the people in other Pacific regions, the Melanesian people are facing problems due to climate change. The effects of climate change are threatening their homes and food supplies, particularly through flooding at high tide and the erosion this causes. In some places, such as the Solomon Islands, many people have already had to leave their home islands and move to higher ground to avoid flooding.

Places like this human-made island in the Solomon Islands are in danger of being flooded.

People living on the islands of Polynesia, Micronesia and Melanesia enjoy rich traditions and histories, which have influenced the art, culture and lifestyles of people around the world. They also share an incredibly diverse range of environments, which the world must come together to help protect.

Our Kokoda Trek

After ten long, hard days, Dad and I have just finished walking the Kokoda Trail in Papua New Guinea. The trail gets its name from the town of Kokoda. It is here that trekkers arrive after a 96-kilometre hike north from a place called Owers' Corner, not far from the city of Port Moresby.

Map of the Kokoda Trail

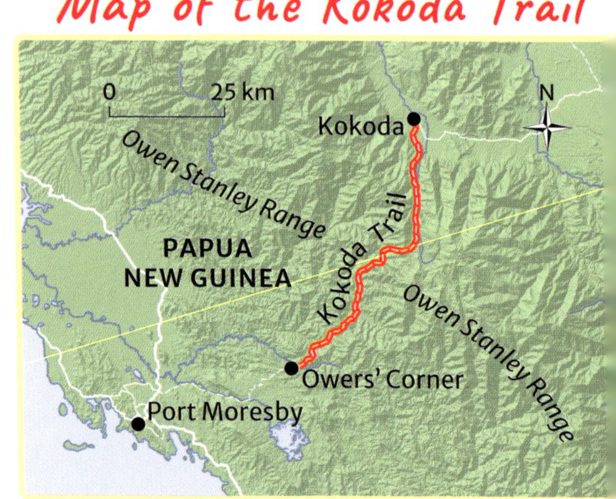

Dad has always wanted to come here, to retrace the steps of his grandfather, who was posted here as a young soldier during World War II. During the war, thousands of Papuan and Australian soldiers fought here to stop an invasion of Japanese forces. Since then, many people have come to honour these soldiers.

The Kokoda Trail is a very long and difficult path through the hilly jungle areas in the Owen Stanley Range mountains. We walked all day, every day of the hike, and we did a lot of climbing up steep and sometimes muddy trails. It's very hot and humid here, so we had to drink lots of water.

Dad and I walked the Kokoda Trail together.

We went with a group of ten other people, including another girl my age. With the help of our guide, Tim, we all supported each other on our journey. As we went, Tim told us all about the history of Papua New Guinea, the war and the cultures of Papua New Guinea's people. We met many of the local people as we walked. They were very welcoming.

Each night, we set up our tents and shared meals with the group, including our local **porters**, who carried our heavy packs for us.

Some of the trail was difficult to climb, but we supported each other.

I was very glad that we had done a lot of training before we flew to Papua New Guinea, because the trail is very demanding. Luckily for us, many people have done this walk before, so the trail was easy to follow without getting lost. As we walked, I couldn't help but think of the soldiers who had trekked through here during the war.

Along the trail, I saw so much spectacular scenery in the jungle, including creeks and rivers, and lots of Papua New Guinean wildlife. I especially loved the bright green butterflies we saw and the deep green leaves of the jungle.

We saw green birdwing butterflies along the trail.

During our trek, we crossed lots of small bridges, some of which were made from fallen tree trunks bound together with rope. A lot of the ground was muddy, too, so my boots were very dirty after a few days. It was very slow hiking because the terrain was so uneven, and often quite steep. One day it even rained on us, but we just kept going.

For the first few days, I really didn't enjoy being hot and sticky all the time, and my clothes never dried out overnight. But by the end of the trek, I was getting used to it.

Local people in Papua New Guinea helped to move Australian soldiers when they were injured.

Dad was hoping to meet a descendant of the man who had helped his grandfather during the war. As we arrived in Kokoda, Dad showed some of the locals a photograph of the man.

Back in 1942, Great-Grandfather had been wounded and had to be carried to safety on a stretcher. The local people did a lot of the hard work, moving injured soldiers away from danger so they could get proper medical help. At the time, the soldiers compared these locals to angels because of the wonderful help they provided.

Sadly, no one we met recognised the man in Dad's photo, but they were very touched that Dad was so interested in this person and his family.

I'm so glad Dad asked me to join him on the Kokoda Trail. I learnt so much about this beautiful country and the people here. I also now understand some of what the soldiers went through during the war. More than anything, I learnt that I am much more **resilient** than I ever imagined! It was a huge challenge, but it was definitely one of the most rewarding things I've ever done.

We stayed in a village in Kokoda once we finished the trail.

Glossary

administered (*verb*)	run or managed by a country
citizens (*noun*)	people who belong to a country
colonisers (*noun*)	countries that take over another country
coral bleaching (*noun*)	when coral turns white as a result of heat or pollution
crust (*noun*)	the outer layer of rock around Earth
currency (*noun*)	a particular country's system of money
diverse (*adjective*)	varied or different
erosion (*noun*)	the wearing away or breaking down of land
hemisphere (*noun*)	one half of Earth, either north or south
hulls (*noun*)	the main parts or bodies of ships
independent (*adjective*)	free from outside control
inhabited (*adjective*)	lived in by people
legislature (*noun*)	a group of people who make laws for a country or part of a country
porters (*noun*)	people whose job is to carry luggage
quarry (*noun*)	a big pit in the ground for digging up stone
resilient (*adjective*)	able to recover quickly
salinisation (*noun*)	when an area is affected by an increase in salt

Index